Laura Seagrave.

KT-488-148

William Heinemann Ltd
10 Upper Grosvenor Street, London W1X 9PA
LONDON MELBOURNE
AUCKLAND JOHANNESBURG

First published 1986
© Allan Ahlberg and Janet Ahlberg 1986
Reprinted 1986 (twice), 1987 (four times)
434 92515 2

Printed in Hong Kong by Wing King Tong Company Limited

# Janet and Allan Ahlberg

# THE JOLLY POSTMAN
## or *Other People's Letters*

HEINEMANN : LONDON

Once upon a bicycle,
 So they say,
A Jolly Postman came one day
 From over the hills
And far away . . .

With a letter for the Three Bears.

Mr and Mrs Bear
Three Bears Cottage
The Woods

So the Bears read the letter (except Baby Bear),
   The Postman drank his tea
And what happened next
   We'll very soon see.

Off went the Postman,
   Toodle-oo!
In his uniform of postal blue
   To a gingerbread cottage –
And garage too!

With a letter for the Wicked Witch.

POSTAGE PAID
2
WARLOCK

THE OCCUPIER
GINGERBREAD BUNGALOW
THE WOODS

OPEN NOW — DON'T DELAY

This could be your lucky day!

FREE
Witch Watch
with every
order

HOBGOBLIN SUPPLIES LTD.
WARLOCK MOUNTAIN
DEPT. 46A.

So the Witch read the letter
  With a cackle of glee
While the Postman read the paper
  But *left* his tea. (It was green!)

Soon the Jolly Postman,
    We hear tell,
Stopped at a door with a giant bell
    And a giant
Bottle of milk as well,

With a *postcard* for . . . guess who?

PAR AVION
VIA AIR MAIL

EAST OF SUN
3¹⁵PM
18 MAY
1986
WEST OF MOON

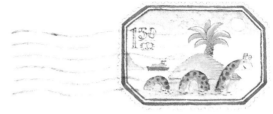

MR V. BIGG
MILE HIGH HOUSE
BEANSTALK GARDENS

FIRST CLASS HOTELS

So the Giant read the postcard
   With Baby on his knee,
And the Postman wet his whistle
   With a thimbleful of tea.

Once more on his bicycle
  The Postman rode
To a beautiful palace, so we've been told,
  Where nightingales sang
And a sign said 'SOLD',

With a letter for . . . Cinderella.
(There's a surprise!)

So Cinders read her little book,
   The Postman drank champagne
Then wobbled off
   On his round again
      (and again and again – Oops!)

Later on, the Postman,
   Feeling hot,
Came upon a 'grandma' in a shady spot;
   But 'Grandma'
What big *teeth* you've got!

Besides, this is a letter for . . . Oooh!

URGENT

B. B. Wolf Esq.
C/o Grandma's Cottage
Horner's Corner

So 'Grandma' read the letter
   And poured the tea,
Which the not-so-Jolly Postman
   Drank . . . nervously.

Now the Jolly Postman,
   Nearly done (so is the story),
Came to a house where a party had begun.
   On the step
Was a Bear with a bun.

But the letter was for . . . Goldilocks.

PLEASE DO NOT BEND

FAR AWAY
20. V. 86.

To
Goldilocks
24, Blackbird Road
Banbury Cross

thdc

So Goldilocks put the pound note
   In the pocket of her frock,
And the Postman joined the party
   And they all played 'Postman's Knock'.

Once upon a bicycle,
     So they say,
A Jolly Postman came one day
     From over the hills
And far away . . .

And went home in the evening – for tea!

The End